Shifty McGifty AND SLIPPERY SAM

For Jean, Peter, and Alfie x
T. C.
For Mum, Dad, and Sherryl x
S. L.

First U.S. edition 2013

Library of Congress Catalog Card Number 2012954337

ISBN 978-0-7636-6838-9

13 14 15 16 17 18 FGF 10 9 8 7 6 5 4 3 2 1

Printed in Shenzhen, Guangdong, China

This book was typeset in Berylium.
The illustrations were done in mixed media.

Nosy Crow
An imprint of
Candlewick Press
99 Dover Street
Somerville, Massachusetts 02144

www.nosycrow.com
www.candlewick.com

Shifty McGifty AND Slippery Sam

An imprint of Candlewick Press

Tracey Corderoy

illustrated by

Steven Lenton

In the dead of night,
when the moon yawned down,
two gloomy robber dogs
plodded through town.

They got to their house, and they flopped down inside.
"We're no good at robbing at all," Shifty sighed.
He tipped out their swag bag,
but nothing was there . . .

except for a spider,
who gave them a **scare!**

"You're right," muttered Sam. "We are bad at this job!
Think of the places we just couldn't rob . . .
the bank and the butcher's, the paper shop too.
The bookshop, the bike shop . . .

and even the ZOO!"

"Hey, we should rob somewhere less tricky," Sam cried.

"Like where?" muttered Shifty. "Where haven't we tried?"

"Our neighbors!" yelled Sam with a whoop and a shout.

"But hang on," groaned Shifty. "They never go out!"

He thought for a moment. "I know what we'll do!
We'll throw a tea party—tomorrow at two.
And **then**, when the neighbors are here having fun,
we'll sneak to their houses and rob every one!"

us

sneaking

"But parties have food," grumbled Sam. "We can't cook."
"Don't worry!" said Shifty. "We've got this cookbook!"

They started with doughnuts, and to their surprise,
they turned out just right, so they cooked some fruit pies.
"Now cupcakes!" cried Shifty. "And let's frost them too!
I never knew baking was fun, Sam. Did you?"

sugar

The party day came, and the neighbors piled in.
"How lovely!" said one with a big curly grin.

They gasped with delight when the food was set down.

"So creamy!"

"So dreamy!"

"The best buns in town!"

"Why, thank you," said Shifty.

"It's nothing!" smiled Sam.

"Would you care for a doughnut

with raspberry jam?"

"Now's our moment," hissed Shifty.
"They're all drinking tea.
We need to get **robbing**
right now — follow me!"

As they sneaked through
the window, they hadn't a clue
that a neighbor had heard
what they wanted to do.

"They're **thieves!**" he said crossly.
"I think that it's time
we all put a stop
to this terrible crime."

As the robber dogs went to see what they could find,

all of their neighbors were creeping behind.

"Oh, WOW!" whispered Sam as they slunk through a door.

They'd never seen so many goodies before!

Then all of a sudden,
the door opened wide.
"No, you don't!"
yelled their neighbors,
bursting inside.

But the Scottie dog suddenly started to sob.
"My teddy!" he sniffled. "They stole Big-Eared Bob!"
"Don't cry," pleaded Shifty,
and Sam turned quite pink.
"We're sorry," they murmured.
"We just . . . didn't think."

"We see now that robbing makes everyone sad.
But we still need a job . . . just a job that's not bad."
"I know!" cried the sausage dog, nodding his head.
"Why don't you open a café instead?"

"A café?" gasped Shifty.
"Do you think that we could?"

"Oh, yes!" cried the others.
"You'd be **really good!**"

So the very next week on the town's busy street,
their new café opened—all shiny and neat.
It had white polished tables
and chairs with pink hearts.
And it served yummy cupcakes
and little jam tarts!

SALES
$2.00

"Oh, wow, Sam," cried Shifty. "Just look at that crowd!
All our neighbors are here. Why, I feel quite proud!"
Sam peered from the window and fluffed up his hat.
"No more robbing!" he said.
"We're done with all that!"

Now Shifty and Sam never grumble or groan.
They **love** baking cakes, and they leave crime alone.
And as for their swag bag,
I'm happy to say . . .

they crumpled it up and they chucked it away!